Katie Woo's

✳ Neighborhood ✳

Best Neighborhood Ever

by Fran Manushkin

illustrated by Laura Zarrin

PICTURE WINDOW BOOKS

a capstone imprint

Katie Woo is published by Picture Window Books,
an imprint of Capstone.
1710 Roe Crest Drive
North Mankato, Minnesota 56003
www.capstonepub.com

Cataloging-in-Publication Data is available on the
Library of Congress website.
ISBN: 978-1-5158-6092-1

Summary: There are so many great things happening in Katie Woo's
neighborhood! Dr. Woo is helping a lot of animals at his vet office. The Sweet
Dreams Bakery is serving up the sweetest desserts. Even the local dentist office
has Katie smiling wide. Read about these neighbors and more in this collection
of easy-to-read stories from author Fran Manushkin.

Graphic Designer: Bobbie Nuytten

Printed and bound in the USA.
002565

Table of Contents

Katie's Neighborhood

Police

Library

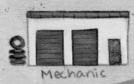
Mechanic

City Hall

Grocery Store

Post Office

Open Wide, Katie!

Katie Woo was at the zoo.

She told her mom, "I love the

alligator. He's so fierce!"

"Look at those teeth," said Katie's dad. "He must need a big toothbrush."

Katie laughed. "For sure!"

"That reminds me," said

Katie's mom. "You are seeing the

dentist tomorrow. The hygienist

will be cleaning your teeth."

"Cool," said Katie. "I love

Ms. Malek."

On the way to the dentist, Katie saw Haley O'Hara and her five brothers and sisters.

Katie told Haley, "I'm going to see Ms. Malek."

Haley said, "Ms. Malek told us we six kids have lost thirty-five baby teeth."

"Wow!" Katie smiled. "That's a lot of visits from the tooth fairy."

Katie and her mom hurried
to the dentist's office. The
waiting room was a fun place,
filled with books and toys.

Ms. Malek greeted Katie
with a big smile. Katie could
see that Ms. Malek was a great
brusher and flosser.

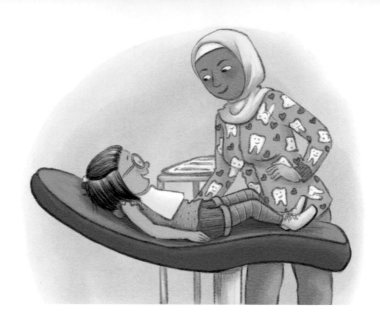

Katie liked taking a ride

in the big blue chair.

"Now, open wide," said

Ms. Malek.

Katie opened wide, like

an alligator.

Ms. Malek used a tiny
mirror to look at each of
Katie's teeth.

"Looking good!" she said.
"I don't see any cavities."

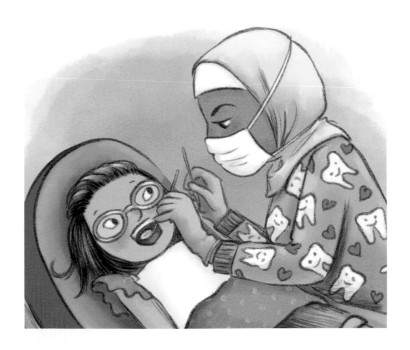

Ms. Malek cleaned Katie's teeth with a cool brush and paste. Katie's smile looked fabulous!

She asked Ms. Malek, "How
do animals clean their teeth?"

"Well, I know what a hippo
does," said Ms. Malek.

"A hippo opens her mouth and a fish swims in. He eats the food between her teeth."

"Ew!" said Katie.

"I'll say!" said Ms. Malek.

Katie's dentist, Dr. Ali, looked
at her teeth too. He told her,
"Next time we will take X-rays."

"Cool," said Katie. "I love
how weird teeth look on X-rays!"

Katie had fun picking a new toothbrush.

"I want pink," she decided. "And cherry toothpaste."

Katie got a toy too.

On the way home, Katie saw Pedro and JoJo. Katie told them about hippos and fish.

"Ew!" said JoJo.

"Gross!" said Pedro.

Pedro told Katie, "The
dentist at the zoo has to clean
the tiger's teeth."

"Wow!" said Katie. "He must
be brave!"

"The tiger is not awake," said Pedro. "The dentist gives him medicine to make him sleep."

"Good idea!" said Katie.

Before bedtime, Katie flossed

and brushed her teeth. She

smiled at herself in the mirror.

As Katie's dad tucked her into bed, she said, "When I grow up, maybe I will work at the zoo and clean the elephant's tusks."

"Wow!" said Katie's dad.

"You like to think big."

"I do!" agreed Katie.

She fell asleep with a big

smile.

The Best Baker

Katie and her friends were

eating cookies after school.

"I'm a great baker," said

Haley.

"Me too!" said Katie.

"Are you sure?" Katie's mom asked. "When you made chocolate cupcakes, they came out hard and salty."

"Oh," said Katie. "That's true."

"I made a birthday cake for my sister," said Haley. "But it fell apart. What a mess!"

Katie's mom asked Haley, "Doesn't your uncle own a bakery?"

"Yes," said Haley. "He works very hard. I'll ask him if he can teach us how to bake."

Surprise! Haley's uncle said he would show them.

On Saturday, Haley's uncle Harry O'Hara met them with a big smile and two aprons.

"Welcome to the Sweet Dreams Bakery!" he said.

Uncle Harry's kitchen was neat and clean.

His cupcake and cake pans were lined up in a row.

"Mom would love this," said Katie.

"I'll show you how to make chocolate cupcakes," said Uncle Harry. "Then I'll make a birthday cake."

"Yum!" said Haley.

"I'll say!" said Katie.

"Here is my cupcake recipe," said Uncle Harry. "It lists all the ingredients. See how carefully I measure them?"

Katie said, "Oops! When I made cupcakes, I just added lots of salt and chocolate powder."

"Not a good idea," said Uncle Harry.

Katie and Haley helped
pour the batter into frilly
cupcake cups.

"Try not to spill any," said
Uncle Harry. "Bakers hate
messes!"

"I'm setting the oven to

the perfect temperature for

cupcakes," said Uncle Harry.

"I also set a timer so I know

when the cupcakes are ready."

"Now I need to bake a birthday cake," said Uncle Harry. "Ms. Malek ordered a big one to surprise her husband."

Uncle Harry sifted the flour.
Then he added eggs and milk
and other ingredients. He mixed
them together.

Haley said, "Now I see the
mistake I made baking my cake.
I didn't mix my ingredients well.
That's why my cake fell apart."

After the cupcakes and

cake were baked, it was time

for frosting.

"This is the most fun,"

said Katie. "I love licking the

spoon."

Uncle Harry began
yawning. "I was baking all
night," he explained. "Bakers
work long hours."

"I'll say!" said Katie.

"Thank you for showing us how to bake," said Katie. "From now on, I will measure well."

"And I will mix well," said Haley.

Katie's cupcakes came out
just right! She brought them
to JoJo and Pedro. They loved
them.

Haley's next cake was also perfect. It made her five brothers and sisters very happy.

But Harry O'Hara was the

happiest person of all.

Why?

Because he loved his work.

And so did everyone else!

Good Morning, Farmer Carmen!

In the summer, Katie and her friends loved going to the farmers market.

Every Sunday they found new foods to taste.

"Come and meet my aunt Carmen," said Pedro. "She's a new farmer at the market."

"Hi!" said Katie. "Is it fun to be a farmer?"

"You can find out," said Aunt Carmen. "Come and stay overnight next Saturday. You can help bring my veggies to market."

"That's cool!" said Katie.

"I'm wild about tomatoes.

Maybe I can help pick them."

"For sure," said Farmer

Carmen.

On Saturday morning, Pedro's dad drove Katie and JoJo and Pedro to Aunt Carmen's farm. It was a long ride.

"Welcome!" called Farmer
Carmen. "Let me show you
around."

Katie saw long, long rows
of lettuce and purple and
green cabbages.

"Uh-oh," said Katie. "I don't see tomatoes."

"Don't worry," said Farmer Carmen. "They are over here. Pick a big one and take a bite."

"Wow!" Katie shouted.

"It's juicy, juicy, JUICY!"

Aunt Carmen smiled.

"My tomatoes passed the

test. They are perfect for

market tomorrow."

Pedro joked, "These cucumbers have goose bumps. They must be cold."

Katie joked back, "They are excited about going to market."

Katie and JoJo helped

Farmer Carmen pick tomatoes.

Pedro liked picking peppers.

He also liked saying, "Pedro is

picking peppers" over and over.

Dinner was a tasty salad.

"Let's go to bed early," said

Farmer Carmen. "We must

wake up at four a.m. to pack up

my veggies to take to market."

It was still dark when Katie
woke up. She saw Farmer Carmen
and her helpers packing veggies
into baskets. They loaded the
baskets onto the truck.

Katie saw the sunrise
as they rode to market.
She yawned and yawned.
"I don't think farmers sleep
very much," she said.

At the market, JoJo and
Pedro stacked up cabbages.
Katie tucked tomatoes into
pretty baskets.

Pedro said, "Aunt Carmen

works so hard. I hope we sell

everything."

"We will," said Katie.

But she was a little worried.

There was so much to sell!

Miss Winkle wanted lots of tomatoes.

Katie told her, "I picked some and packed them."

"Way to go!" said Miss Winkle.

Katie sold carrots to Sharon, the mail carrier. Mr. Nelson got lettuce and cabbage for his grocery store.

But at closing time, many

veggies weren't sold.

"This is sad," said Pedro.

"Very sad!" said JoJo.

"Wait!" yelled Katie.

"Look who's coming?"

It was Haley O'Hara and her five brothers and sisters.

"Yay!" yelled Haley. "We're not too late for veggies."

They filled seven bags. No veggies were left!

Katie told Farmer Carmen, "You work very hard!"

"But my work is tasty," said Farmer Carmen. They shared the last tomato.

It was very tasty!

Katie's Vet Loves Pets

"*Meow! Meow! Meow!*"

A kitten was crying. Katie

saw her hiding under a bush.

The kitten was alone.

"You need a home," said
Katie. "When Dad comes back
from work, I'll ask him what
to do."

Katie's friends skated by.
She told them, "This cat needs
a home."

"I already have two cats,"

said JoJo.

"I have a dog," said Pedro.

"My dad is allergic to cats."

"I want a big fluffy poodle,"
said Haley. "But my mom says
six kids are enough for one
small house."

When Katie's dad came home from work, he said, "This kitten is very sick. She may die. We can't take home a sick kitten."

Katie asked her dad,

"Can we take her to the vet?

Dr. Wong saved Pedro's dog

when he was sick."

"All right," said Katie's dad.

"Let's try."

Dr. Wong's waiting room
was filled with pets.

Miss Winkle was holding
her dog, Twinkle. "He comes
for his shots every year."

Katie's friend Barry was with his iguana.

"Zorba is sick," Barry said. "He hasn't been eating his broccoli. Zorba loves broccoli!"

Roddy was with his parrot,

Rocky.

"I'm worried," said Roddy.

"Rocky stopped talking. He

always has something to say!"

Katie and her dad went in to see Dr. Wong. He picked up the kitten.

He looked in her ears and her eyes and her mouth.

"You came just in time," said Dr. Wong. "This kitten has a bad infection. I'll give her medicine to help her feel better."

Dr. Wong told Katie, "You must give your kitten medicine every day."

Katie looked at her dad.

"*Is* she my kitten?"

"Yes!" Her dad smiled.

"Yay!" Katie hugged her dad.
Dr. Wong told her, "Your
kitten should be feeling peachy
in a week or two."

"*Peachy!*" said Katie. "That's a perfect name!"

"A very cool name," agreed her dad. "She's the same color as a peach."

Dr. Wong said, "Some pets do not get well. They are too sick or old. That makes me sad. But most of the time, my job makes me happy."

Katie told him, "I hope you can help my friends' dog and parrot and iguana."

"I'll try," said Dr. Wong. "I love all the animals."

Katie told her friends, "Meet my new kitten, Peachy."

"Peachy! Peachy! *PEACHY!*" said Roddy's parrot.

"You are talking!" yelled Roddy. "You are *not* sick!"

Katie took good care of
Peachy. Every day she gave
the kitten medicine and food
and lots of love.

Peachy got
better and
better. So did
Barry's iguana.

Roddy's parrot
could not stop talking!

Katie could not stop talking too. She told her friends, "Dr. Wong will always help us keep our pets well."

And he did!

More About
Dental Hygienists

Where they work: in a dentist office

What they do: Dental hygienists clean and x-ray teeth. They also teach patients how to take care of their teeth.

What they wear: Dental hygienists wear uniforms called scrubs. They consist of pants and a shirt.

More About Bakers

Where they work: in bakeries, restaurants, or grocery stores

What they do: Bakers cook baked goods such as breads, cakes, and cookies.

What they wear: Many bakers wear a chef jacket and pants.

More About Farmers

Where they work: on a farm, either outside or in barns and other farm buildings

What they do: Farmers raise crops for human food or animal feed. They also raise animals for food or other products, like wool, for example.

What they wear: Farmers wear comfortable clothes that are made out of strong, durable materials.

More About Vets

Where they work: in vet clinics or in animal barns on farms

What they do: Vets give medical care to animals.

What they wear: Many vets wear scrubs, consisting of pants and a shirt. Sometimes they also wear a long white jacket called a lab coat.

About the Author

Fran Manushkin is the author of Katie Woo, the highly acclaimed, fan-favorite early reader series, as well as the popular Pedro series. Her other books include *Happy in Our Skin*, *Baby, Come Out!*, and the best-selling board books *Big Girl Panties* and *Big Boy Underpants*. There is a real Katie Woo: Fran's great-niece, who doesn't get into trouble like the Katie in the books. Fran lives in New York City, three blocks from Central Park, where she can often be found bird-watching and daydreaming. She writes at her dining room table, without the help of her two naughty cats, Chaim and Goldy.

About the Illustrator

Laura Zarrin spent her early childhood in the St. Louis, Missouri, area. There she explored creeks, woods, and attic closets, climbed trees, and dug for artifacts in the backyard, all in preparation for her future career as an archeologist. She never became one, however, because she realized she's much happier drawing in the comfort of her own home while watching TV. When she was twelve, her family moved to the Silicon Valley in California, where she still resides with her very logical husband and teen sons, and their illogical dog, Cody.